P9-BXV-014

5/10

MT. PLEASANT PUBLIC LIBRARY
MT. PLEASANT, IOWA

DEMCO

# Wiggle Giggle Tickle Train

# Wiggle Giggle Tickle Train

MT. PLEASANT PUBLIC LIBRARY
MT. PLEASANT. IOWA

Nora Hilb and Sharon Jennings

with photos by Marcela Cabezas Hilb

annick press
toronto + new york + vancouver

©2009 Nora Hilb (concept and illustrations)
©2009 Sharon Jennings (text)
Design: Sheryl Shapiro
Photographs by Marcela Cabezas Hilb, with the following exceptions from
iStockphoto Inc.: sun, car, pony, moon ©Robert Simon, ©Ian Hamilton,
©Ernesto Solla, ©Don Joski.

Annick Press Ltd.
All rights reserved. No part of this work covered by the copyrights hereon
may be reproduced or used in any form or by any means – graphic, electronic,
or mechanical – without the prior written permission of the publisher.

We acknowledge the support of the Canada Council for the Arts, the Ontario
Arts Council, and the Government of Canada through the Book Publishing
Industry Development Program (BPIDP) for our publishing activities.

ONTARIO ARTS COUNCIL
CONSEIL DES ARTS DE L'ONTARIO

Cataloging in Publication

Hilb, Nora
    Wiggle giggle tickle train / Nora Hilb, Sharon Jennings.

ISBN 978-1-55451-210-2 (bound).—ISBN 978-1-55451-209-6 (pbk.)


    I. Jennings, Sharon  II. Title.

PZ7.H5375Wi 2009        j813'.6        C2009-901100-X

The art in this book was rendered in watercolor.
The text was typeset in Zemke Hand.

Distributed in Canada by:    Published in the U.S.A. by:
Firefly Books Ltd.    Annick Press (U.S.) Ltd.
66 Leek Crescent    Distributed in the U.S.A. by:
Richmond Hill, ON    Firefly Books (U.S.) Inc.
L4B 1H1    P.O. Box 1338
    Ellicott Station
    Buffalo, NY 14205


Printed in China.

Visit Annick at: www.annickpress.com

For my sisters Claudia and Vera,
who wiggle, giggle, and tickle my life.
—N.H.

To Drew and Rory Brannon.
—S.J.

Up with the sunrise,
color it bright.
Dazzle and sparkle, such fiery light.

# GOOD MORNING!

Train's in the station,
pulling out fast.
Wiggle and giggle and tickle and laugh.

CHOO-CHOO!

Jump in and paddle,
webbed feet can dabble.
Splishing and splashing and waddling say . . .

QUACK!

Zooming and vrooming,
we won't slow down.
Faster and faster we're racing around.

# HONK!

Hold on to the saddle,
pony might prance.
Bucking and frisky, he's roaming the ranch.

GIDDY-UP!

Tongue gives a wiggle,
tooth gives a wriggle.
Grin with a gap as you say peekaboo.

SMILE!

Jet planes are roaring,
wings flung so wide.
Gleaming and climbing and touching the sky.

FLY!

Tap is drip-dropping,
hear it plink-plonking.
Water goes splash as it spills from the jug.

# OOPS!

Candles are glowing,
frosting is sweet.
Gooey and ooey and yummy — let's eat.

# BLOW!

Paper boats floating,
put out to sea.
Sailing or rowing, the captain is me.

AHOY!

Gallop or canter,
horse likes to trot.
Clippety-cloppety-clippety-clop.

NEIGH!

Bedtime for baby,
safe in our house.
Lullaby, rockaby, shushaby,

# HUSH!

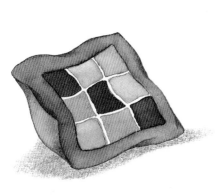

Cut out the bright moon,
hang it with thread.
Shimmering, glimmering, over my bed.

# SLEEP TIGHT!